Which way should I go?

Dedicated to my beloved husband Martin,
and all my family members, friends and all the people who have helped me with this book.

Published in 2012 by Simply Read Books | www.simplyreadbooks.com
Text & Illustrations © 2012 Vanya Nastanlieva

Library and Archives Canada Cataloguing in Publication

Nastanlieva, Vanya
The new arrival / written and illustrated by Vanya Nastanlieva.

ISBN 978-1-927018-13-2

I. Title.

PZ7.N375Ne 2012   j823'.92   C2012-903679-X

We gratefully acknowledge for their financial support of our publishing program the Canada Council for the Arts, the BC Arts Council, and the Government of Canada through the Canada Book Fund (CBF).

Printed in Malaysia

Book design by Heather Lohnes

10 9 8 7 6 5 4 3 2 1

He searched through sunny meadows,

under dark bushes,

He checked everywhere.

It was almost perfect, except...

Sam was happy.

I haven't seen him around.

Who's this stranger?

Soon he found a wonderful place to live.

Little Sam set off to find his.

There once was a hedgehog named Sam.

When you are little hedgehog,
even a few weeks old,
you must find your own place to live.

It was a perfect day.

And when the day ended and the sun started to fall,
Sam knew that he had found the perfect home.

It was a welcome party just for him.

He met many new friends, ate
lots of food, and played fun games.

Sam even got a present to keep
him warm until his quills grew in.

Nice try!

Hey!

Oh dear!

Come on! We're late!

OUR WOODLAND!

WANTED: A FRIEND

HEDGEHOG AT THE HOLLOW TREE

SAM'S PLACE

Nice to meet you! - - - - -

Hello! -

WELCOME TO

There was a big surprise for him!

In the morning,
Sam went back to his
lonely home, where...

But that night there
was a terrible storm.

All his notes were blown away,
and his quills too.

"With no notes and no quills,
I will never find a friend,"
Sam thought.

and another...

He used his broken quills
to pin up a note.

Then he plucked out more quills to pin up another one...

...he landed on his head and broke some of his favorite quills.

And that gave him an idea.

Sam didn't give up. He had ups

Nor did the heavy rain...

But he still couldn't find anyone to play with.

Strong winds didn't stop him.

and around big trees.